MW00891619

# Gilroy's Goof

Doug and Debbie Kingsriter

Illustrated by Ann Iosa

WORD PUBLISHING
Dallas · London · Vancouver · Melbourne

**Our thanks to:**
Laura Minchew for believing that
all of us need to care for God's Earth;
Laura Minchew and Brenda Ward for creating this
book series to encourage little and big people alike
to do what we can to be good stewards of our world;
and all the children who are teaching us, by example,
to take care of God's beautiful earth.

***Other Books in the***
***Save God's Earth Series:***

*Clipper's Crazy Race*
*Finny's Big Break*

***Gilroy's Goof***



**Library of Congress Cataloging-in-Publication Data**

Kingsriter, Debbie, 1951–
Gilroy's Goof / by Debbie and Doug Kingsriter; illustrated by Ann Iosa.
p. cm. — (Save God's Earth)
ISBN 0–8499–0922–8
I. Kingsriter, Doug. II. Iosa, Ann, ill. III. Title. IV. Series: Kingsriter, Debbie. 1951– Save God's Earth
PZ7.K618Gl 1992
[E]—dc20

92–12580
CIP
AC

Printed in the United States of America

2345679 LBM 987654321

*To our children,*
*Lauren, Barrett, and Blake,*
*but especially Blakey, whose little feet and*
*trusting eyes call us to protect the earth that he*
*will grow to inherit*

Gilroy the Gopher was the biggest problem in Walkers Woods. Now it wasn't because he was unfriendly. Gilroy was very friendly. He had a wonderful smile. And it wasn't because he was lazy. Not Gilroy. He worked very hard. But that was where he goofed. He worked *too* hard.

You see, Gilroy loved to dig. He tunneled through more earth in a day than most bulldozers. And because he liked to dig so much, Walkers Woods was full of tunnels. And *that's* what made everyone unhappy.

One day the squirrels Chit and Chat couldn't find the acorns they'd saved in the hollow tree. That's because the acorns had fallen into a tunnel underneath their tree.

Chit was really upset. “This is Gilroy’s tunnel!” said the little squirrel.

“Let’s find him and tell him what for!” yelled Chat.

Just as they started out, a jogger came by. Suddenly his foot caught in a gopher hole, and he went crashing into the hedge. He almost hit Snowshoe, who was taking a nap.

“Ouch! Crazy gophers,” muttered the jogger as he rubbed his ankle and hobbled away.

Snowshoe the rabbit turned an angry red. “That does it! I’ve had it!” she hollered. “I know gophers like to dig, but Gilroy’s ruining everything.”

Suddenly out of the hole popped Gilroy's happy face. "Did someone call me?" he asked innocently.

"Why do you have to dig so much?" demanded Snowshoe.

"Because I'm a gopher," replied Gilroy with a big, friendly smile. He thought everyone liked his tunnels.

"You're wrecking our woods," Snowshoe said in a loud voice.

"How about digging somewhere else for a change?" Chat asked.

"Okay, I'll dig in the garden then," said Gilroy. He flashed another big smile and disappeared underground.

The garden was next to Walkers Woods. Michael and Meredith Brant were weeding their flowers and vegetables.

"We're going to have a great garden this year," Meredith said excitedly, "especially if we can keep the animals out."

“Yeah, and I think these cans are gonna do the trick!” said Michael. He was stringing cans together to make a fence. “The noise these cans will make ought to scare them off.”

When the can fence was finally in place, Michael stepped back to admire his work. "How does that look?" he asked.

Meredith stopped weeding the last row of carrots to look at Michael's fence. "Looks pretty good," she said. "Let's go make lunch. I'm hungry." Michael tossed the extra cans into the woods, and together they hurried toward home.

By mid afternoon Gilroy had tunneled his way to the garden. He was anxious to see what there was to eat. KA-BONK! His head hit something hard. Gilroy dug his way to the top to see what it was. There he saw the shiny cans strung around the garden. His head had hit the stake holding the string. Then he saw some bright colored cans on the ground right in front of him.

"All right!" said Gilroy. "Something to eat!" He opened his mouth and took a big bite. SCRUNCH! Gilroy's bite made a terrible noise. But the pain was even worse.

What had he done? His teeth and jaws hurt terribly. Tears came to his eyes. Slowly he crept back toward his tunnel. But the thought of digging made him stop. It would hurt too much.

So with his head down, Gilroy carefully walked back to Walkers Woods. He saw more cans strewn along the path. *Those are dangerous,* he thought. *I've got to warn my friends.*

Gilroy found Snowshoe and the squirrels Chit and Chat. "How come you're not digging?" asked Chit.

Gilroy could barely move his sore mouth. "I bit into one of those shiny things," he said, pointing at a can. "We have to get these things out of the woods, before someone else gets hurt."

Chit, Chat, and Snowshoe looked at each other. Then they looked at Gilroy. "Maybe some other day," yawned Chat.

"I've got some other things I have to do," said Snowshoe. Then they scampered off in different directions.

"This is a terrible day," moaned Gilroy. "I can't dig, I can't chew, and now my friends won't help me." He began to feel downright sorry for himself.

Ophelia Owl heard the whole thing. She flew down and put her wing around Gilroy.

"Having a tough day?" she asked.

Gilroy looked up, trying hard not to cry. “I got hurt, and my friends weren’t even sad about it, Ophelia.”

“I think they’re upset with you because of where you dig,” said the Owl.

“I thought they liked my tunnels,” replied Gilroy.

“Not when your tunnels hurt them,” Ophelia said softly. Gilroy shook his head.

The Owl continued. "When God made the earth and people and animals, He had a great plan for looking after them."

"What's that?" Gilroy asked.

"He wanted each of us to take care of what He created. Problems start when we don't show respect for God's creation."

"How?" Gilroy asked.

"Like digging tunnels that ruin gardens and hurt others. Or throwing cans where they don't belong," replied Ophelia.

"Do you think I should stop digging?" asked Gilroy. He was afraid the Owl's answer would be yes.

"No, but you should be more careful *where* you dig," responded Ophelia. "And you need to tell your friends you are sorry for the trouble you caused. Then after you help clean up the mess you made, they might help you with the cans."

"Thanks, Ophelia. You're a good friend," said Gilroy with a tiny smile. His mouth was starting to feel better.

Gilroy found Chit and Chat at their hollow tree. They were trying to figure out how to make their acorns stay in the tree. "I'm sorry I caused your acorns to fall," Gilroy said. "I'll fill up the hole, and I'll never dig near your tree again."

Chit and Chat smiled. "Thanks Gilroy! I hope your mouth gets to feeling better soon," said Chit.

"Me, too," said Chat. "I miss your big smile."

Gilroy felt much better. Suddenly his face brightened. "Say, I've got an idea," he said. "You want to hear it?"

When the Brant kids returned from lunch, they saw that part of their can fence was down. “It’s that gopher again,” said Michael as he pounded the stake into the ground.

“Look at this!” exclaimed Meredith. She was pointing at the marks on the can Gilroy had bitten.

“That ought to keep him from coming around here,” said Michael.

"I'm not sure these cans are such a good idea, Michael," warned Meredith. "This must have really hurt."

CLANK. CLUNK. A can bounced behind Michael and Meredith. "Hey, who threw that?" shouted Michael, looking toward the bushes. "Show some respect, will ya?"

In the tree above, Chit and Chat smiled. Then Michael and Meredith heard a noise from the edge of the woods.

"Look, there's that crazy gopher!" pointed Michael. Meredith and Michael watched as Gilroy nosed the cans away from his tunnel entrance. They were the same cans Michael had tossed away earlier that day.

Michael spoke first. "Meredith, I think you're right. We should take the can fence down," he said.

"Good," said Meredith. "And we should pick up any other cans we see, too. They don't belong in the woods."

"I'll go get a recycling bag, and we can start right now," said Michael as he headed for home.

In no time at all the children had filled the bag with cans and trash. "Pretty good start, huh?" said Michael as he wiped his forehead.

"Sure is," smiled Meredith. "Let's do this again tomorrow. We'll make Walkers Woods the prettiest ever."

Behind the bushes, Snowshoe began a happy thumping with his foot. Chit and Chat gave each other high-fives. And Gilroy? Well, he just smiled and smiled.

Gilroy's big goof helped everyone learn something that day. The children learned that recycling shows respect for God's earth and animals.

Gilroy learned to be more thoughtful about his friends' feelings. And his friends—Chit, Chat, and Snowshoe—learned to forgive him and . . . to appreciate how fun it is to have a friend with a great big smile like Gilroy's!

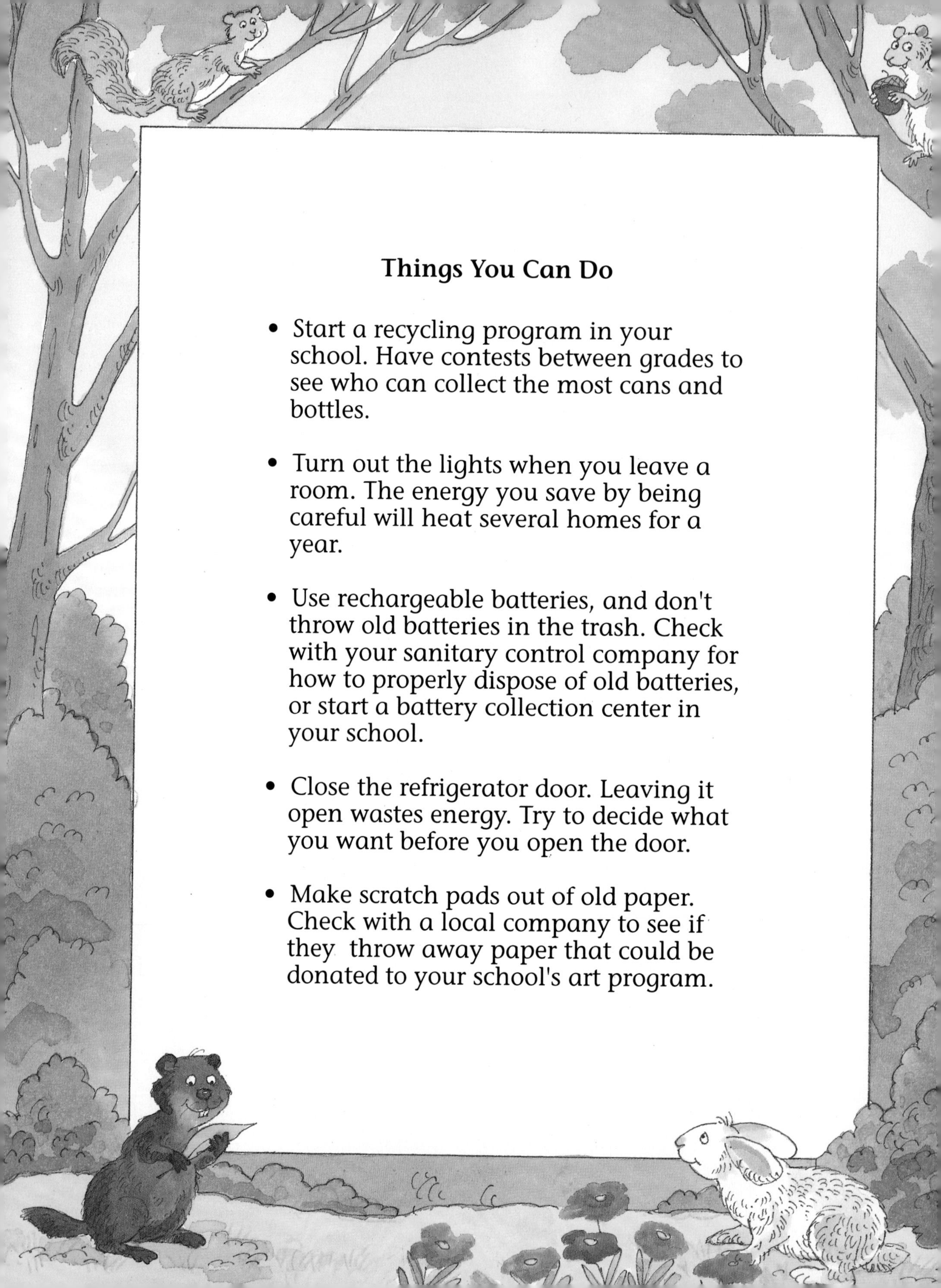

## Things You Can Do

- Start a recycling program in your school. Have contests between grades to see who can collect the most cans and bottles.

- Turn out the lights when you leave a room. The energy you save by being careful will heat several homes for a year.

- Use rechargeable batteries, and don't throw old batteries in the trash. Check with your sanitary control company for how to properly dispose of old batteries, or start a battery collection center in your school.

- Close the refrigerator door. Leaving it open wastes energy. Try to decide what you want before you open the door.

- Make scratch pads out of old paper. Check with a local company to see if they throw away paper that could be donated to your school's art program.